T0383504

**For Oliver and especially Lara
for loving dinosaurs!**

First published 2018 by the Natural History Museum, Cromwell Road, London SW7 5BD
Reprinted 2020, 2022
Text and illustrations © John Hamilton, 2018
www.johnhamiltonartist.com
Layout © The Trustees of the Natural History Museum, London, 2018
P10, drawing of cat on the wall by Lara Hamilton

ISBN 9780565094591

A catalogue record for this book is available from the British Library

10 9 8 7 6 5 4 3

Reproduction by Saxon Digital Services
Printed by Toppan Leefung Printing Limited

The girl who really really really loves Dinosaurs

John Hamilton

Published by The Natural History Museum, London

It is fair to say
that Lara is MAD
about dinosaurs.

Lara wears NOTHING but her dinosaur costumes.

She even has special dinosaur
outfits for all her dolls
and teddies.

And Lara's pet cat Bob has his own dinosaur outfit. Lara calls him ...

Bobasaurus!

But what Lara really, really,
REALLY wants is a pet dinosaur
all of her own.

The first place
Lara decides
to look is the
museum.

She finds a T. REX
among the dinosaurs
but thinks ...

'Oh no! He's far
too big and bony.
I would not like
him for a pet.'

'This one is a bit too scary.'

'And he
is far too
spikey!'

Lara decides to explore the rest of the museum.

She looks at all the other animals
and notices that many of them
have similar features
to dinosaurs.

Finally, Lara comes to the birds

and finds out some interesting facts ...

Dinosaurs laid eggs like birds.

The T. rex and the chicken have similar shaped skulls.

T. rex also had very similar feet to birds.

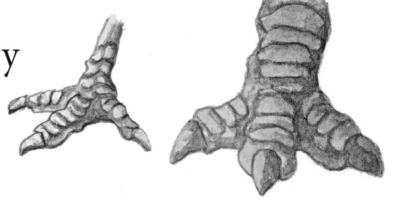

AND it might have had feathers!

In fact birds, such as chickens, are the closest living relatives to the dinosaurs!

So now …

Lara has her own dinosaur world in her garden! And it is fair to say that she really, really, REALLY loves birds!